BEING BRAVE

A Book about Being Afraid

CAROLYN LARSEN
ILLUSTRATED BY TIM O'CONNOR

BakerBooks

a division of Baker Publishing Group
Grand Rapids, Michigan

Text © 2017 by Carolyn Larsen
Illustrations © 2017 by Baker Publishing Group

Published by Baker Books
a division of Baker Publishing Group
P.O. Box 6287, Grand Rapids, MI 49516-6287
www.bakerbooks.com

Printed in the United States of America

Library of Congress Cataloging-in-Publication Data
Names: Larsen, Carolyn, 1950– author.
Title: Being brave : a book about being afraid / Carolyn Larsen ;
    illustrated by Tim O'Connor.
Description: Grand Rapids : Baker Books, 2017. | Series:
    Growing God's kids
Identifiers: LCCN 2016032804 | ISBN 9780801009747 (pbk.)
Subjects: LCSH: Fear—Religious aspects—Christianity—
    Juvenile literature. | Fear in children—Juvenile literature.
Classification: LCC BV4908.5 .L36 2017 | DDC 179/.6—dc23
LC record available at https://lccn.loc.gov/2016032804

Scripture quotation is from the *Holy Bible*, New Living Translation, copyright © 1996, 2004, 2015 by Tyndale House Foundation. Used by permission of Tyndale House Publishers, Inc., Carol Stream, Illinois 60188. All rights reserved.

17   18   19   20   21   22   23   7   6   5   4   3   2   1

Don't be afraid, for I am with you.
Don't be discouraged,
for I am your God. I will strengthen
you and help you. I will hold you
up with my victorious right hand.

———

ISAIAH 41:10

See that boy? That's Max. He tries to be a brave boy but the truth is he gets scared sometimes.

My name is Leonard and I'm Max's favorite toy.

Mom!" Max cries. "Mom!"

"What's the matter, Max? You should be sleeping," Mom says.

"I can't sleep. I'm scared," Max says.

6

"Why are you scared?" Mom asks.

"There are scary things in the dark," Max says.

"It's going to be okay," Mom says. "Let's pray. That always helps me when I get scared."

Max is afraid of what he can't see. That's why he is afraid of the dark.

Being afraid isn't bad because it sometimes helps Max be careful.

Praying helps Max remember that he is never alone. God is always with him.

Don't be afraid.
Isaiah 41:10

Max is scared. He has to go to the doctor today to get a shot. That means the doctor will stick him with a needle.

Max does not like needles. He does not even like to think about needles. He is scared that the shot will hurt a lot.

"Do I have to go?" Max asks.

"The shot might hurt for a little bit," Mom says.
"But it will help you stay healthy. You can hold
my hand while the doctor gives you the shot if you
want."

Max grabs Mom's hand and squeezes it tight while the doctor gives him the shot. It hurts a little, but Max knows it will help him.

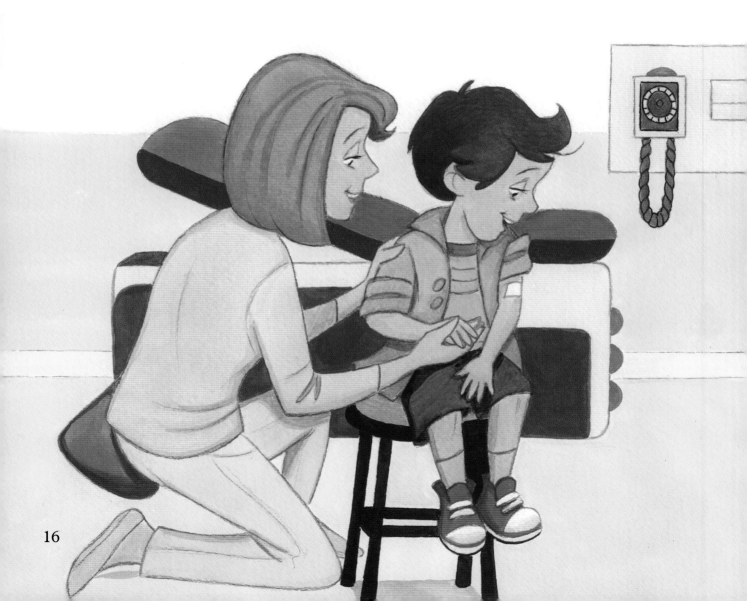

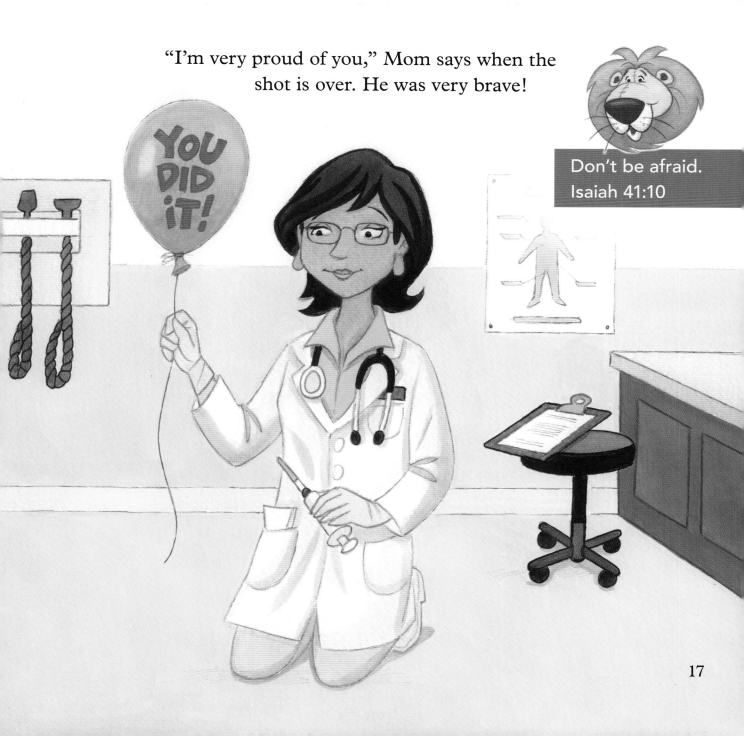

"I'm very proud of you," Mom says when the shot is over. He was very brave!

Don't be afraid.
Isaiah 41:10

Look how dark the sky is," Max says. "Is there going to be a storm?"

"The weatherman said there are thunderstorms headed this way," Mom says.

"What are we going to do? What if our house blows down?" Max says.

Max is scared of storms. Loud thunder frightens him. Flashing lightning makes him jump. The wind blows hard and sometimes the lights go out.

Max hides in the closet. He just wants the storm to be over.

"Max," Mom says, "storms can be kind of scary. But we are in a safe place."

Mom and Max thank God for a safe place to stay during a storm.

Don't be afraid.
Isaiah 41:10

Max's dad got a new job. But the job is in a new city. Their family has to move.

Max is scared to move. He is scared to leave his friends, to go to a new school, and to live in a new neighborhood.

What Max is really afraid of is change. He is scared that he won't make new friends. He is scared that he won't be happy in their new town.

Max has to go with his family, but he is scared.

"I'm scared," Max tells Dad. "How will I make new friends?"

"New things can be scary," Dad says, "but they can also be very exciting. Let's think of fun ways you can make new friends."

Don't be afraid.
Isaiah 41:10

29

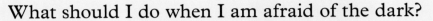

What should I do when I am afraid of the dark?

1. Learn a Bible verse about God protecting me.
2. Get a night-light to keep on in my room.
3. Make a list of happy things to think about while I'm falling asleep.

What should I do when I'm afraid of the doctor?

1. Remember that the doctor wants to help me stay healthy.
2. Squeeze someone's hand or think about happy things.
3. Ask God to help me be brave.

What should I do when I am afraid of storms?

1. Remember that even storms are under God's control.
2. Ask God to help me be brave.
3. Respect the power of storms by staying in a safe place.

What can I do when I am afraid of new experiences?

1. Talk with my parents about what scares me.
2. Ask God to help me be brave.
3. Come up with a plan to face whatever is scaring me.

Remember

God says I am never alone. He is always with me.

God loves me. He will help me through whatever scares me.

New experiences can be scary but they are good too. I will learn new things and grow stronger in my faith in God.

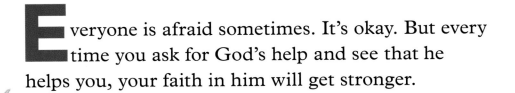

Everyone is afraid sometimes. It's okay. But every time you ask for God's help and see that he helps you, your faith in him will get stronger.

Don't be afraid.
Isaiah 41:10